For Momo

THANK YOU

Mom and Rob
Anna and Stefan
Carine France, Andrea Clark, Yalitza Ferreras
Betty Bigas, Ben Zweig, Erin Klenow and Arjun Gowda

First published in 2018 by Whippstein Press
1044 Revere Avenue, San Francisco CA 94124

Book production & project management by David Brimble.
Color reproduction by Red Reprographics Ltd, London.
Printed and bound in China on FSC® assured paper.

ISBN 978-1-7323554-0-8

WHEN I WAS BIG AND YOU WERE LITTLE

a book by RS Whipple

It was bedtime.
But Pina wasn't having it.

Little Pina pleaded.

Big Dad had other plans.

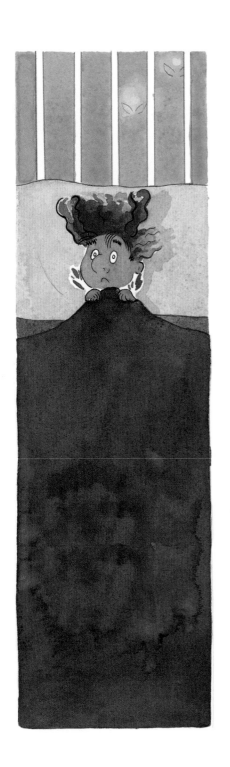

Still, Pina had a sinking feeling.

I will not fall asleep, thought Pina.
I will NOT fall asleep.
I will not. Faa...
faa...faaaalll...

Bop!
Pina bounced from bed to floor.
She had a most peculiar sensation.

Her dad was little. And Pina?
Well, Pina was...

BIG.

When I was big and you were little
we went for long walks at night.
Down the unbound staircase,

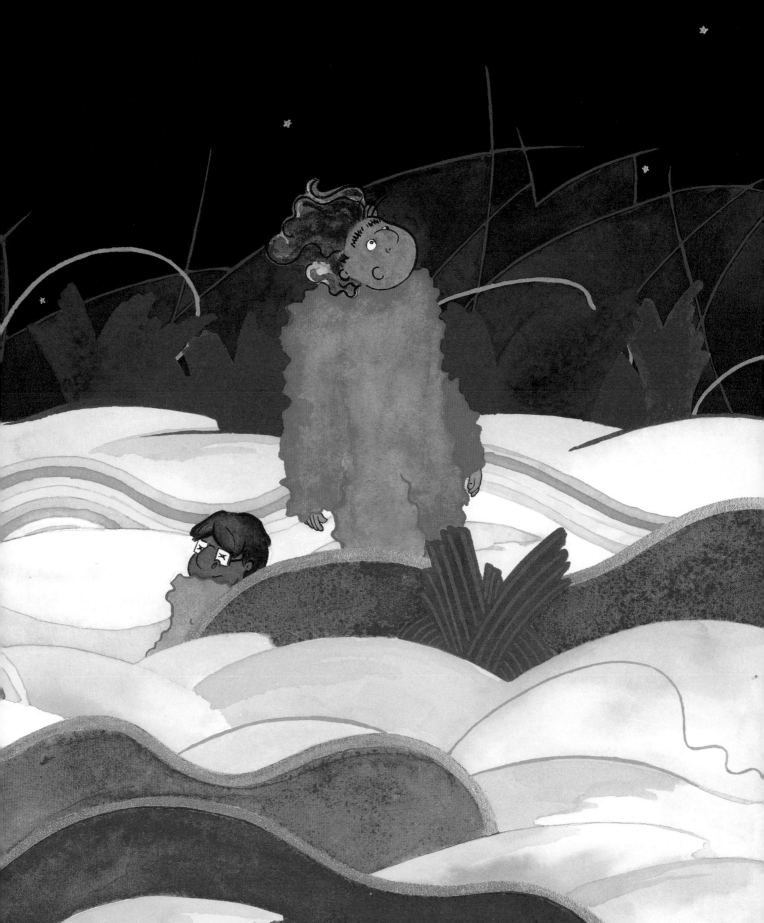

through walls of whispering grass,

into the soggy spider basin,

and onto a churning brook,

past the midnight fruit fighters,
ducking berries left and right,

to dance at the great beaver dam.

Then Little Dad yawned, and Big Pina blinked.
It was time for bed.

But Little Dad's face scrunched tight.
What's wrong? asked Big Pina.
I don't want our adventure to end,
sighed Little Dad.

Little Pina had an idea.

They tromped out the bedroom door,

into the starlit room,

and Little Pina,
and Big Dad,
built one giant bed,
with room for two –

and a few snuggly friends.